# Love, Love

Victoria Chang

STERLING CHILDREN'S BOOKS
New York

An Imprint of Sterling Publishing Co., Inc.
1166 Avenue of the Americas
New York, NY 10036



ISBN 978-1-4549-3832-3

Distributed in Canada by Sterling Publishing Co., Inc.
c/o Canadian Manda Group, 664 Annette Street
Toronto, Ontario M6S 2C8, Canada
Distributed in the United Kingdom by GMC Distribution Services
Castle Place, 166 High Street, Lewes, East Sussex BN7 1XU, England
Distributed in Australia by NewSouth Books
University of New South Wales, Sydney, NSW 2052, Australia

For information about custom editions, special sales, and premium and corporate purchases, please contact Sterling Special Sales at 800-805-5489 or specialsales@sterlingpublishing.com.

Manufactured in Canada

Lot #:
2 4 6 8 10 9 7 5 3 1
03/20

sterlingpublishing.com

Cover design by Heather Kelly
Interior design by Heather Kelly and Julie Robine

# LOVE, LOVE

VICTORIA CHANG

STERLING CHILDREN'S BOOKS
New York

# Table of contents

To all the bullied kids in the world: I see you.
To all the kids who suffer: I see you.

And

To my human children: Penny and Winnie
To my wiener dog children: Mustard and Ketchup

# 1:

# missing

## See

I see my sister Clara on
the ground in the back
of the school

I see a few kids around her
at least I think it's her

I see a dirty window
dirty kids
dirty yard
everything dirty

especially near the end of winter
when the snow picks up all the mud on
the ground and

mixes it all up
I love snow but only snow

snow always sucks up
the earth in
this cold dirty city

West Bloomfield Michigan
there must be blooming fields west of here

all the flowers keep
sprouting in my head

when they pop out of my head

the city pulls them out like weeds

after school I ask Clara

*were you at*
*the back of the school today*

she snaps

*no that wasn't me*

*on the ground*

# The Disappearing Wig

Clara's new wig is gone
that's all I know

that's all anyone knows

I didn't know anyone knew
about the new wig

Clara's first wig

Clara's only wig

but maybe it fell off
by accident

maybe that's when someone took
it or maybe someone
knew about the wig and pulled
it off her head no one

tells me what happened no one
is crying I just hear my

mom's angry Chinese to

my dad downstairs

the next day
Clara is wearing
a navy blue beret like the French
do or at least I think

they do because
I think the word is French I think

she should put on a striped shirt
walk a white poodle

and paint a moustache above her lip

people don't make fun of the French
like they make fun of the Chinese

when the French speak
flowers come out
of their mouths

when the Chinese speak
it sounds like arrows

sometimes people pull
their eyes to the
corner to make them small and beady

what would it be like to see

the world through two
small slits

I should know

but I don't

# The Chins

Clara is my older sister
I'm Frances
we're the Chins

the same as the one on a face

I know little about Clara
beyond the basics

I'm 11 and she's 12 almost 13
we're only 14 months apart
born in Detroit Michigan

I know my lips pout and go
out and down
hers stay in

I know I never
listen to my parents
she always does
I know that in

pictures her hands
are always together in the front

and she never smiles

sometimes
I can't keep my laughter
tucked under my clothes

sometimes questions swirl
in my brain like a tornado

I know I'm supposed to be
a bug that tiptoes on my
hand that

I can see
but can't

hear or feel

but I know
I'm not

# Winters

We live where my parents' jobs are
my mom is a high school
math teacher in Detroit

my dad is an engineer at
Ford Motor Company in Dearborn

they also own a Chinese restaurant
of course it's called *Dragon Inn*

our state is shaped like a hand

people always hold their right hand up and
point to a spot to
show where they live

people sometimes lift their left hand first
then have to switch

Michigan is freckled with lakes but
we don't ski we don't ice-skate
we don't go boating

my parents don't
know how to do these

things we probably don't have
money to do these things

*for lao mei* says my mom
for Americans

she says
*too dangerous*
about everything

she lets us eat at McDonald's sometimes
and eat pizza because

my dad loves hamburgers
and she loves bread

in the wintertime

nothing moves

if you look closely
the smoke from all

the chimneys rises
one inch at a time

in the winter the snow

covers everything

eventually mutes us with its
beauty and

whiteness

# Books

My parents won't buy us
anything but books

books books books
everywhere in all shapes
everywhere all the time

Clara reads mostly Nancy Drew
she reads them over and
over and over again

whenever I try and touch
them or read them she grabs

them back or yells at me

*mine, don't touch*
she always says

my mom won't buy any
Nancy Drew for me because

*no doubles, waste of money*
and because Clara is older
she gets everything first

once in a while when Clara isn't
looking I take one I know she's

just finished and read it with
a flashlight under my
covers at night

my favorite Nancy Drew book
is *The Clue of the Leaning Chimney*

because there are
Chinese people in it

I try and read as fast as I can
so I can put the book back
the next day

those days at school I'm so
tired I feel like I'm walking
in a gray cloud

# The Secret in *The Secret of the Old Clock*

Up in the corner
on page 3 of Clara's
Nancy Drew book
*The Secret of the Old Clock* is

a small piece of
hair stuck to the paper by

the tiny bulb of a tiny root
the hair is only around

one centimeter long as if
someone has lightly drawn a

little line on the page with a pencil
and put a little dot on the end

I don't want to

touch it but it stares back
at me daring me to ask questions

thc words on the page

blurred all I can see is
the little

black line

another on page 6 another

slightly longer on page 8
another on page 11

two on page 14 stare

back at me

calling me in

calling

me

in

# No One

No one can figure out why
Clara's hair keeps falling out

I find more and more pieces all
around the house mostly in

books but also on
the bathroom counter

on the floor
in the car

Clara's bald patch isn't

all bare but takes up the
top of her head
a big oval littered with

bits of hair all tiny
short one-centimeter pieces that

stick straight up

wanting to grow long trying
to grow long but

unable to grow long

no one can figure out
why no one else can figure out why

her hair is falling out
everyone else thinks someone

else should know

maybe the

full moon made her hair fall out

maybe she is an alien

maybe the snow makes
her hair fall out

why does
Clara's hair insist on

leaving

its country

# Wig Shop

Just two weeks ago
we had gone to the wig shop

bodiless white Styrofoam heads
everywhere

brown wigs

blond wigs

the sign said some

were made of real hair
I shivered
thinking some of these might

be from dead people

*the black wigs are*
*in the back*
said the woman after
she looked at us

Clara and I wandered

the store on our own
she on the other side I on

my own side

I put on the blue wig
ran to Clara and posed like
a dancer

*you look stupid*
she said
*you're gonna get lice*

she was in one of her moods again

maybe because this was
our first time
in a wig store

maybe because this would be her
first wig

I never know what mood
Clara will be in

it's not like
walking on eggshells

more like

walking on a field of grenades with
snowshoes on

the woman came back

with a bobbed wig all black
as black as a black hole

Clara tried the wig on
my mom's nose covered with
sweat beads
her face flushed

the sales lady's eyes two holes

voices from a TV somewhere

the lady explained how to
care for the wig
how to put it on

I moved towards the front of
the store waited for

the cash register to

open then close

*that's expensive*
I heard my mom say

# Pin by Pin

The new wig had
worked well

it almost
looked like my sister's hair
just a little thicker and blacker

each morning
she put it on her head like a
motorcycle helmet

she pinned the lining of the wig
into her real hair
what was left of it at least

it was a slow process

pin by

pin

sometimes I glanced at her as I walked
by the bathroom careful not to
turn my head

pins in her mouth
hand stabbing black little
sticks into her head

no more swimming

no more roller coasters

no more convertibles

no more

hanging upside down

no more

sky

diving

## The Missing Wig

Clara goes shopping for
more berets I wonder if
she'll get another wig or if

she likes being French
I wonder if

she will take French class
I wonder
why she doesn't get a blond
wig instead
she can pretend she's

an American
a real American

a white American

I begin to wonder
where her wig went

everyone else seems to

have forgotten
about it I want to know where
it is I begin to wonder who

took it

I miss the wig

its smells
its thick blob dripping in
the wind while drying

I want the wig back
it covers

up everything

so well

# Stories

I don't get wigs or hats or
berets

instead my mom gives me

a new diary
it's silver and says

*Perfume* on the cover
each page smells like

what I imagine
a pretty French
woman's
neck might smell like

I can almost see
my reflection on the cover

sometimes I play with Barbies

make up stories and write
them down in my new diary

*I can't believe*
*you still play with Barbies*
Clara says

I tell her *there's no one*
*else to play with*

she just
looks at me
shrugs

goes back to her room

when I play with my Barbies

someone
always loves

someone who

doesn't love
them back

## My Mom's Car

I see my mom's car outside when
I'm walking back to

class from the bathroom

why is she here
is it about Clara on the
ground at school

am I in trouble what
did I do I'm sure

I'm in trouble
my face gets warm like
a light turned on in my
head by
someone else

I can't find
the off switch

I take my
time because I'm

scared of my sixth-grade teacher Mr. Heart
he yells at our class a lot

his voice bellows and pricks me
like needles

I can hear it
in other
parts of the school too

but when I'm in his room it feels different

the difference between watching
the snow fall and being in

the snow

if you are in the snow you
are cold and wet

but watching the snow from
the inside is beautiful

you're supposed to do it with
a mug of hot chocolate around

a crackling fire hugging your family
laughing and sharing stories

at least that's

what the books say

no one calls me into
the office

no one tells me why
my mom is here

nothing

silence

# Talk

I speak perfect English but
try not to speak at school

when someone speaks to me
I just answer and

look down
sometimes kids laugh and say

*AH SO you no speak Engrish*

people talking is like music

I listen
to the music from the
outside and it always sounds pretty

but I can't play any instruments
maybe I can

learn by listening by seeing
other people's lips go up and down

side to side

*speak up more* my dad says
*talk more like the Americans*

he tells us how
he's learned to speak up at work

but I don't know how
to be like him

everywhere I turn I am

different everything
we do is
different my mom tells me

*don't be like the Americans*
*they brag too much*
*talk too much*

I don't know who I'm
supposed to
believe

# Neighbors

Our neighbors are
mostly American mostly Jewish

so I think Jewish and
American are the same

the Rubins live
diagonal to us

Josh is the younger boy

his mouth is slightly crooked
he has an endless
tan on his face
he has curly
brown longish hair

something
mean about the way he rolls up

his snowballs and looks
in my eyes before

he throws them
the snowballs little

white fists of

ice and
cold

# The Birds

At school I'm especially
scared of

Josh Rubin and
Steve Zucker

they follow me
say *chink* and
*hi ya* as they slice the air
with their hands and squat

they call me *fried rice*
and *egg roll*

in PE we run
around the field every Friday

my heavy body feels
like a wheelbarrow

Steve follows me
runs by my side

turns around and runs
backwards
his arms swing hard
he's facing me
laughing

his blond curls
bounce in
the air
his mouth covers
a lot of
his face so that
he looks like a frog

*you're SO SO ugly*
*open your eyes*
he laughs with his fingers pulling
his eyes to make

them squinty

I used to be

lanky laughing

now my hair is

thick and short I wear plastic
glasses with pink frames

my face puffy like a chipmunk
skin stretched out greasy

my mom buys my clothes
and I think they look funny

I button my shirts at the top
like she tells me to

I think my pants are too short

at least she doesn't use mothballs

I know my clothes look different from
other people's clothes but

I don't know how exactly
most days I feel bruised and blue

I know I don't look good
I know people don't think I look good

I know I'm not popular or
likeable

other kids watch Steve yell at me

most kids glance at me
look away
their eyes sorry and
filled with pity but
pity has no legs
pity is pitiful
still
useless

others linger like Josh

whose eyes stare right
at me
into me

my hands shake and I feel like
I'm running on stilts

my eyes hold in the tears as if
I'm running with a full cup of
water that I don't want to spill

I ask the birds to
come help me

the birds are free
I wish I could go up and
down like them

today their calls sound like shrieks they

circle but don't

come

down

## Sally Levin

Sally Levin finds me crying in

the locker room after PE

*are you okay*

she sits down on the bench
her body like a small wet heater

I can't answer because the tears

burn
in my chest
my heart too busy swelling in

its wetness

her question makes me
cry the endless kind of
tears the ones that aren't
meant for anyone to see

I want her to leave me alone

I want her to stay with me I want

to tell her something
about my fists that don't only

clench and the broken birds
inside my chest

but I don't know where
to begin so

I don't
begin

at all

# Tennis

Sometimes I bring a tennis racket
and a container of old balls
to the park

I always put my phone on
the ground near the back fence

just in case my mom calls
even though she should know
where I am since I come here
all the time

It's the only time I take my
phone out

it must be so lonely always
in my backpack

it's a hand-me-down from Clara
everyone at school has newer
better shinier phones

not me never me

mom always calls when I'm
on the other side picking up
balls and I have to run

all the way back and pick
up her call

It's always the same thing
*dinner soon, come home*

But before she calls
I know I have some time
and I hit balls against
the tennis wall

the harder I hit
the harder the ball comes
back to me

if I hit too low the ball comes
back too low
but I can bring it back up with
my racket
if I hit too high the ball bounces
too high back
but I can bring the ball back
down with my racket

my body powerful
swinging feels like
a big wave
powerful and fluid

sometimes I pretend
the bald balls are
Josh and Steve and hit
them as hard as I can
but they keep
coming
back

sometimes I hit back and forth
with the wall until it's so late

the ball

turns

into

night

# Jogging

Today while jogging during
PE class

I hear *wig* and

I want to get closer
but I don't want to get closer

Josh and Steve say it again
maybe they called me a *pig* maybe I

should stay
away from them

then I hear it again

*wah wah wah wig wah wah wah*

so I speed up and linger behind
them just far enough away

*where did you put it*
Josh says

*in the back of the fence*
*wah wah wah over there*
Steve points ahead to the back corner
of the field

Josh turns around

his eyes like two large clocks
*what are YOU staring at*

they speed up and
run away laughing

I run through
clouds of dust from their shoes
my ears are

dusty
my ears stand tall

I stand
a little taller

# A Good Plan

I mark the corner of the field with
my eyes and memorize

the bushes where I think Steve's
finger was pointing
but I can't get over
there without our PE teacher Miss Beeoh
seeing me

I decide to go
later during a bathroom break right

before Mr. Heart begins to
scream at us

I'm good at knowing when
that is

when his mood begins to

detach from his body

and the mood

travels across the room and the
ceiling begins its lowering

I don't have to ask to
go because I'm mostly

*a good kid*

the good ones
can go on their own

I'll go later to that spot near the fence

that's a good plan

that's the first plan I've ever had

the first
best plan

I feel strong

I now have ideas

that can

fly

# Bathroom Break

As I guessed

Mr. Heart is
ready to blow up

this time it's because
we all failed a test

he's passing the tests back and
muttering louder and louder

*I'm disappointed in all of you*

I jump up and grab the

bathroom pass and start walking
kind of jogging
down the hall

by the time I get to the end I can
hear him screaming

I look around and
push open the door
the chilly wind rises around

me as if I'm near a plane's
propellers

the birds swerve above and
come into

a circle around me they
follow me as I race to the
edge of the yard my
heart pricks my

chest with every beat

as I run faster it begins to
slap my chest

I am home out here

I can be me out here
all the trees root

for me as they spread
as far as they can in the

wind and snap back
to their original positions as if

clapping

something is going to happen

the fields are

blazing

## The Wig

I look around the area
Steve had pointed to
I dig through

the tall grass and the bushes
I want so badly to
find the wig to
be the hero to

be someone
important to be heard
to be seen
I look and look

I keep hearing

the birds and
the trees
the leaves touching each

other always touching each other

I want so badly to find the wig
my head is

filled with screams
the screams are
fighting with each other are

screaming at each other to
stop but I can't find the wig anywhere

maybe it blew away
maybe the birds took it for a nest

maybe Steve moved it maybe I never
heard them talking about it

maybe there was never a wig
maybe I don't live in Michigan
maybe I'm going crazy

a group of birds explodes out of
a tree from a scream it's

Miss Beeoh

# No Wig

I have no wig and I'm in
trouble too

my mom arrives

I don't say anything

I have nothing to say

the birds in the trees took all

my words with them

in the car on the way home
my mom scolds me in Chinese
she's crying

*you embarrassed me*
*you need to focus on school*
*we came to America for you*

all I can do is look at
the ketchup stain on the seat
and how it's spread and dried into

the shape of a wingless bird
how it can never change never fly away

I look at the clouds in the sky making
new shapes
expanding and shrinking

a cloud can disappear
that means the clouds in the sky

are always new ones I've never

seen before
new ones beginning
again and again

let me

begin again

too

# 2:

# the beginning of something

# Annie

Annie lives in my
neighborhood she's
my only friend

her parents are Chinese too
she's a grade younger than me but
it doesn't matter

because she's a grade younger
I hardly see her at school
but it doesn't matter

I don't eat lunch with her
at school but it doesn't matter

I can't wait to tell her
about the missing wig

she'll understand
she'll know what to do

we understand

the sky in the same way

we understand the moon

in the same way

we ride our bikes in the forest

where the sun's rays look like
ribs through the trees

the forest is our body

Annie always smells like swamps and
butterflies her hair always
looks like silly string

she carries a notebook around

draws pictures of turtles and
whales and of
robins and rabbits

she has big eyes that droop and
when she laughs

her whole body shakes

## Tennis

Some days Annie and I bring
our rackets and old balls to
the tennis courts

between her mom calling and
my mom texting
sometimes we are running

all over the court
back and forth back and
forth

she stands past the baseline
and I in front of it because
I hit much harder

*you should join the tennis team*
*at the bubble*
she always says panting
after we hit
*you're so good!*

I've never gone into
the bubble but
I know it's a bunch
of tennis courts covered
by a huge white cloth
and it looks like a big bubble

playing tennis with Annie
is so fun even though
most of the time I'm
running back and
forth to reach
her balls that zig and
zag out of bounds

we laugh so hard
our cheeks hurt

I'm strong only on the tennis court
I'm brave only on the tennis court

my large body serves with
weight and force

nothing can

stop me when

I have

a racket in

my hand

# Mystery

I'm not sure what I heard
about the wig anymore because
ideas have a way of

going into my brain
turning left and right and

then I'm not sure of anything

I wonder how girls like
Sally Levin walk so

straight up every day

I slouch more every
hour at
school

what I think I know fades
like a flying bird's call

but on the tennis court
words come out
of my
mouth like a
fast
river

I tell Annie about
the missing wig

*we need to do something*
she says
*we have a mystery to solve*

I'm scared but
I know Annie's right
Annie's always right

*you be Nancy Drew and*
*I'll be Bess*
I say

*no no YOU'RE Nancy and I'm Bess*
she says
and I don't
argue with her

## A Stranger

Once a woman stops
our hitting and invites me
to the bubble to try
out for the tennis team

her name is Coach Meredith
*you have such a natural swing*
she smiles at me
*I could help you*

I'm too scared to say much
but I nod

she keeps watching us
for a while and
I feel the little dogs in
my stomach jumping
up and down

I hit a few more balls
into the net than normal
but Coach Meredith
doesn't yell at me
she just
gives me some
pointers

I don't know

anyone

like her

# The Hill

On our way home from
tennis that day
Annie and I ride our

bikes up and

down

our favorite hill

we ride up the hill out
of our saddles

our rackets slung
over our bodies

tennis balls moving in our
baskets like popcorn

we swing our bikes right and left
right and left

we zoom down the hill
tucked into our handlebars as

fast as we can go

our smiles stretched across
our faces by
the cold wind

*let's go no hands* Annie says

*I don't know* I answer

*it'll be fun* she pushes my
forearm

*well okay* I say even though

my hands are shaking

she goes down first
her hands by her side

bike zigzagging

then she lifts her arms up
like an eagle

she stops at the bottom and
waves

my turn

I breathe in deeply and

close my eyes imagine
that I am about to hit a tennis ball

I start pedaling and slowly
take my hands off the bars
the bike is so wobbly
I think I'm going to fall off
I lift my hands into
the air the wind tries to stop me
but I go faster and
faster the bike steadies
this is what
it means to fly
Annie is jumping up
and down clapping
I nearly hit her
as I pass her
I am so
proud
there is
confetti
exploding
inside
me

# Focus

When I get home
I tell my mom about
the tennis team

and how maybe I should
try out

*tennis is a waste*
*of time*
she says with her back
turned

she's cooking and
all I can hear are
vegetables screaming
in the pan

*focus on your schoolwork*
*it's not good to copy*
*Americans*
*too much sports*

I feel a seed of anger
in my stomach
and I want so badly to

say something back
to yell something back

but the phone rings and
the seed in my

stomach stays
shut

# Hair Dream #1

In my dream, Clara's hair wraps around the house, crawls into the windows. The hair suffocates me. I can't breathe. I want to cut the hair into thousands of little pieces. Then I am on the edge of a waterfall of hair. I am in a boat about to fall down. I wonder if the hair will make a splashing noise when I fall. I wonder if I will break into a thousand pieces like confetti.

## Clue Collecting

On a Friday with no school
Annie convinces me
to bike the two miles to
find the wig

we know we'll get in big
trouble if anyone finds out
it's too far and
there's a busy road

bits of leftover snow rest at
the side of
the road and look like

big dirty teeth

I wish I had paid more
attention to the school bus route

luckily Annie is good with
directions and only gets us
lost four times

we must look funny
two Chinese American girls
riding on the side of
the road at the end of winter

sometimes a car honks a long
honk so the sound moves from
behind us and doesn't stop
until it is far ahead like
a long string

hopefully no one will
recognize us

my bike zig

zags like my

heart

# Bushes

When we finally get to school
we both breathe out deeply

I show Annie where I think
Josh and Steve pointed to but
I'm not
sure anymore

all the bushes look
the same
why do they all
have to be so green

these bushes are
stubborn and greedy

they keep all their leaves each winter

Annie starts digging through
the leaves with her hands

I start on the other side

opening up each

bush like

a present

# Wet Wig

Before Clara's wig was
stolen our mom

washed it once a week
because it always started to smell like
dirty hair but not

exactly dirty hair but
fake hair on top of dirty

hair the wet heavy blob

sat on a chair
resting in the winter sun blowing
just like the trees

I wondered

whether it was happy to
finally be left alone

bodiless again

or was it happy to be
on my sister's hot head

I think she hated the wig
itchy smelly
afraid it would

fall off but I think the wig

loved her

must have loved her must have
wanted to serve her

as a service dog might

love its owner

# School

I have no idea how
long we've been digging

I take a break and stand up straight
to stretch my back that has
been bent like a table

our school from afar
looks so small

a miniature building
gray and rectangular

so silent now
so empty now

it's hard to believe

so much

happens in that

tiny building each day

it's a whole

city in

a box

I see the kindergarten building and
its butterfly garden

where I used to fly up
and down in circles
following the butterflies

once in kindergarten
my mom picked me up
her eyes inked

with tears

she said
*you have a big mouth*
*you talk too much*

I had told the teacher that we had
the same workbook at home
my mom was called in
scolded by
the teacher

I told the truth
I thought I was supposed to
trust the teachers I didn't know

how to lie didn't want
to learn how to lie

my mom's eyes
in the rearview mirror

looking back at

me looking at the road

yelling crying *I am trying*
*to help you*

*you have to be smarter than*
*them work harder than them*

*that's the only way you're going to*

*make it here because*

*you will never*

*look like them*

# Double

Clara was always in the Gate
Program for gifted kids

not me

when others asked my mom about us
she always said Clara is

*the smart one*

she laughed when they
asked about me

*Frances is always playing*
*with Annie*
*always going to the park*
*always playing tennis*

*always wasting time*

I'm always the youngest in my grade

Clara is always the oldest in her grade

we don't speak to each other at

school we survive
on our own we know

that it would be worse if we
banded together

double target

double Chinese

double

bad

luck

# Dance

Even the PE building looks
small from here

Miss Beeoh
makes us dance in that
building

slow

dance

I wonder how slow dancing is
exercise but I never dare
to ask

Miss Beeoh is athletic and tall with
short brown hair

she always makes us stand up one by
one to pick our partners

her mouth a dark line on her

face the corners curl up just a little

sometimes the boys pick the girls
sometimes
the girls pick the boys

I always hold my breath as each boy

stands up walks around and looks at
the girls like they are shopping

my brain always in a partial dark sleep
like a fish

the boys always laugh and
snicker when

they pass me

Miss Beeoh always stands with her arms
crossed

the line on
her mouth and its

endless curling

sometimes if a boy is absent
I am usually

the last one left sitting on

the side wearing a
cream-colored gym suit with
three green stripes down the sides of
each pant leg

tight from my
thunder thighs

short and faded from too many
washings

my face always

heavy with shame
some stared and laughed

others looked away
as if I were contagious

once during dance
I got to pick first
I picked the
Chaldean boy named Henry who was
always the last boy

everyone laughed

Marci said *of all people you*
*pick Henry?*

the whole time Henry didn't look
at me his hands felt soft and moist

I wanted to tell him that *I'm sorry*

and that I picked him because
we're about the same size
and I thought he wouldn't
laugh at me

but his face was red like the center
of a bull's-eye

he didn't

thank me

# Searching

*What are you looking at*
Annie asks

*nothing*
I say as I realize
I've been resting

for too long
thinking for too long

I get back to digging
in the bushes

I keep digging
until my hand brushes against

something soft

something that

feels like

hair

a soft raspy sound

comes out of my

mouth

# Maybe

Annie runs over just as I'm
pulling the branches apart

down at the bottom
a small clump of
yellow twigs and grass

in the middle are a bunch of
almond-shaped gray ears

tiny dark eyes that look like
watermelon seeds

the heads and bodies all tangled
together curled in

strange positions that look
uncomfortable

*BUNNIES*
Annie and I scream

the little brown gray bunnies twitch
at our yelp
we know better than to touch
them but want to grab
each one and squeeze as hard
as we can

*LOOK*
I point to a part of their nest that
has some long
black strands

we both guess what

that means

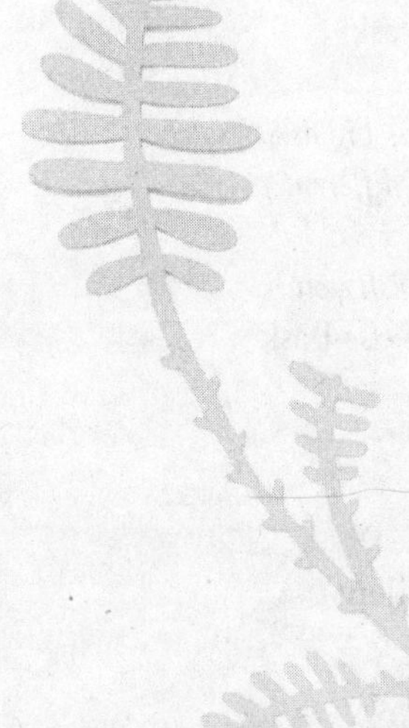

# Happy

We get back to the bushes
pull them apart

dig

dig

dig

we must be close

eventually we take a break to
eat our snacks

*do you ever wish you lived somewhere else*
I ask Annie

*all the time* she says
*I wanna go to California someday*

*what's there* I ask

*beaches trees as big as skyscrapers*
*different stuff different people*

*do you ever wish you*
*were someone else* I ask

*all the time*
she says

then she is silent

she doesn't ask me
because we both
know my answer too

now I've spoiled

our happiness

## Nothing

We get back to searching but

can't find the wig

and the sun is already hanging in

mid

air

like a giant red mole on
the sky's face

we peek one more time at
the bunnies

we get on our bikes
pedal home so full of

California and
bunnies

in our

hearts

that we almost forget about
our failed

mission

almost

# Hair Dream #2

In my dream, my mom learns how to make my hair into a bun. For a week I leave the bun up, even during my showers and I feel like a warrior. I flex my muscles in front of the mirror. On the eighth day when I release the bun a thousand doves fly into the sky. They tell me that they're flying to California and ask if I want to go. When I say *yes,* they overlap their wings and carry me across the prairies on a magical white carpet. Everything is white. Even my hair has turned white.

## *Chinese School*

The next day is Saturday
and Saturday means

Chinese School
where we drive
an hour to

meet with all the other Chinese
people who
drive hours

to meet with all of us
we take
Chinese language classes taught by

our moms and dads we
write calligraphy

sometimes I wonder what my schoolmates
are doing on Saturday mornings

I wonder whether they would

laugh at me now

there are a hundred of us
half here half nowhere half surviving
half drowning

this Saturday
I can't stop thinking about
the wig

where is the wig
where is the wig

WHERE IS

THE

WIG

we practice a
sword dance for
the yearly show we giggle

in our crouched
poses swords up

our costumes with sleeves so wide a
small poodle could fit in there

my sister dances
slowly and carefully

she's wearing a beret today
there must be ten bobby pins to

hold her beret down

somehow I'm etched into these other

people I see once a week
but I'm not
sure how

I keep forgetting the moves

keep stepping on my own
sleeves

*concentrate Frances*
yells Mrs. Wu

but I can't focus

all I know is that

this is taking away my
sleuthing
time

# From

Like my parents
most people at Chinese School are
from a place

really far away called Taiwan
people always say

*I know where Thailand is*

I'm not sure where either is
exactly but I've gone to

Taiwan before

I just don't remember

my mom is originally from
mainland China the big country

that looks like Mother Goose
she left there during a war and ended
up in Taiwan
people sometimes ask me

where I'm from and I say *Michigan*
they always shake their heads

*no where are you from from*

I think they mean Taiwan and China
can I be from somewhere I've
never really been
I always nod and smile

because they seem to know what
they are saying and I don't

question them

other times people say

*my brother's wife's sister-in-law's cousin married*
*a Chinese lady from Taiwan*

I wonder if she is really from
Thailand

# Dragon Inn

This Sunday like many
Sundays

I sit in the last booth in the
back of my parents' restaurant

stuffing fortune cookies into
wax bags
for the takeout orders

Clara is sitting across from me
stapling the bags shut

she's wearing a white
baseball hat

it's dirty at the edges that touch
her hair

her eyebrows look cross

as she pushes the stapler down
each time

it's always

quiet

here

I want to ask Clara
about the wig but know
she will just yell

at me

instead I ask
*do you want an egg roll*
*I'm gonna make one*

*no*
she says not looking up
as she staples

I've been eating too many
egg rolls again

everything is sticky at the restaurant
the seats are sticky the walls

sticky the saltshakers sticky
when I walk into the kitchen

my shoes go *crunch*
*crunch crunch* so

there's nowhere to hide

except the bathroom

but big red cockroaches scatter down
the sides of

the bathroom walls
their antennae twitching

they have so much confidence
act as if they own
this place
belong
here

I hear a scream in the bathroom

I bring a plate

of almond cookies to
the screaming guest

and smile

# The Apartments

After we finish the egg roll bags
my dad brings us to

the apartment buildings that

they own with a bunch of
Chinese friends

my dad wants to *make it big*
he rubs
his hands together

today we paint the
insides and fix up empty apartments

I roll up and down wiping
off drips that slip
down the wall like little tears

ideas about finding the wig

bloom in my head

they sprout like
little moles that pop out

of the ground

I grab each one
and hold it tightly

I can't wait to see Annie
and tell her

about my ideas

I'm like my dad
full of new ideas

but I'm not brave
like him

once he and a man were
speaking loudly

I heard the man say
*that's not how we do*
*things in this country*

*go back to where you came from*

my dad waved his arms up and
down as he yelled something

my mom pulled him

back into the apartment

after that my dad
didn't speak

painted over

the electrical outlets so
thick with

layers you could barely
see the holes when

he was done

# New Idea

After a long weekend of working
I finally get to meet up
with Annie at

the tennis courts

we volley to each other
so we can hear each other

I tell her about my new idea
*what if we write a note to*
*Josh and Steve*

Annie volleys a ball back
*like a ransom note*
*I like it*
*but you write it*
*you're better at it*

I glow at Annie's compliment and
volley another ball back

*how about this* I say

*we know what you did*
*give back the wig*
*by Sunday March 16*
*under the big rock that leans*
*3pm or else*

*or else what* Annie asks as
she bends down for a ball

*I don't know*
I shrug

I've never threatened
anyone before

at school
I write up the note twice
and we slip it
into Josh's and Steve's desks

then we wait

# Deadline

Our deadline
comes and

goes we check every day
for a week after, too

*they're not scared of us at all*
sighs Annie

*I know*
I say
*we have nothing they want*

*that's it* she says
*what if we give them something*
*they want*
*like a trade*

*MONEY*
we both say

when I get home I collect all
the money I have and add it up
it totals $6

the following day
Annie gives me $10

I write another note
this time remembering to
add Laurel Park

I wonder if they didn't know

which rock we were talking about

*leave the wig under the big rock*
*in front of the school where people talk*
*by Sunday March 30 midnight*
*and for doing it right*
*you will find a ton*
*of money with a 6 and a 1*

we hope they'll think it's

$61

not $16

## Light

We both regret saying
midnight because we can't
sneak out of the house

but *midnight* rhymes
with *right*

so Annie asks to
sleep over and our moms
actually say *yes*

it's our first sleepover
the other kids at school
have had tons of
sleepovers by now
but not us

we stay up and look out
the window with my
binoculars

around 11:30 I feel
a hand shove my shoulder

it's Annie

a small cone
of light outside

skitters across Josh's yard

then the light moves down the
street suspended

as if someone is riding a bike

we are so excited

we no longer

feel sleepy

# Money

On Monday Annie hands me
a clump of blond hair in
a clear sandwich bag

*the money's gone*

I touch the hair
hold it up
look at it

*this is Barbie's hair*
I say a little too loudly

*now what*
Annie says

we don't hear the closing and
opening of the metal lockers
all around us

someone bumps into me so
hard that I drop the hair

it scatters all
over the floor as if
we are at a hair salon

except our hair

would be

black

## Deflated

Annie and I don't talk
about the wig anymore

all our excitement
all our hope
leaked out like hot air out
of an old window in
the winter

how are we ever going
to find the wig

if only we could see
the bunnies again

collect the happiness

wrap the happiness in a blanket
bring the happiness home

open the blanket when
we need the happiness

when people say
happiness is
within us
maybe they mean

memory

like the memory of

the bunnies

and the soft fur that

brushed my hand

maybe

# 3:

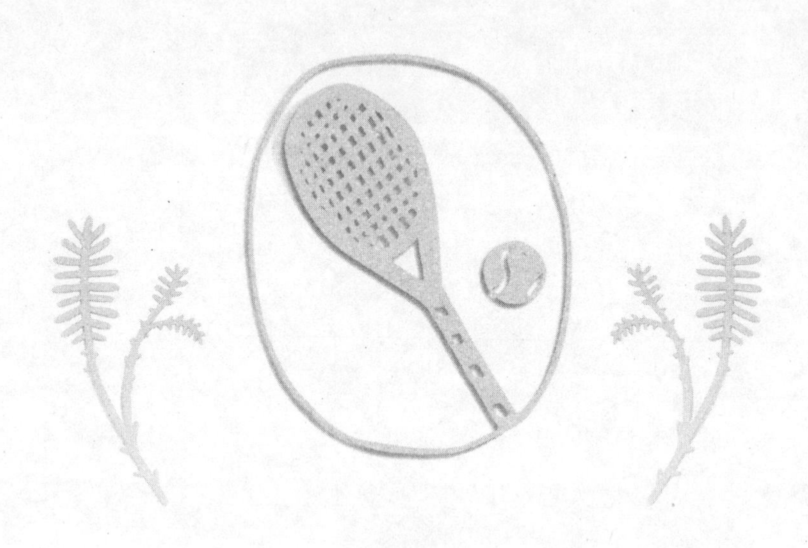

# maybe

## New Plan

Even though Annie and I didn't
find the wig

it stays in the back
of my head like an

empty hanger at the
end of a closet

*maybe we can*
*figure out*
*why Clara's hair is*
*falling out*
Annie shouts
while she tries to hit
one of my tennis balls back
but can't

*nice topspin*
she gasps

*thanks*
I say back
then I shout
*HOW*

she walks to the net to
pick up a ball with her
ankle and racket
*I don't know*

I say
*maybe I'll start spying more*
*at home*

*don't forget*
*to take*
*lots of notes*
she says as she
tosses a ball to me

*it's your serve*
*but be nice*
she laughs

I serve and it's an ace
in the corner
as if it's a sign

that our plan
is a good one

# Fix It

My parents are arguing
about Clara's hair again

*stop talking so loudly* my mom says in Chinese

I sit at the top
of the stairs with my
notebook and pen

my dad says in English
*it will stop falling out if she wants it to stop falling out*
*she can fix it*
*we can fix it*
*she needs to exercise more*

*that won't help* my mom says

my dad says something
about doctors

*American doctors don't know anything*
my mom says

I hear the garage door open and
slam shut
my dad is almost
done drilling the snap-on
buttons for the curtains in the van

he's changing our van into a
travel van so

we can drive across

the country and see everything

*see America the Beautiful*
he says

my mom is sewing brown
velour curtains that

cover all the windows so

no one
can see in

# Hair Dream #3

In another dream, I brush my hair before leaving for school, one stroke down after another but one stroke brings down a huge clump of hair as thick as a horse's tail, then another, and another, until I'm bald.

# Haircuts

My dad is cutting Clara's hair
because she doesn't

want to go out to get her
hair cut

she doesn't want
anyone
to see

they sit on the deck
Clara has a towel around
her neck my dad slowly and
carefully trims

the back of her hair to a bob
he always cuts it a little

too short they always
pick the least windy days
when the sun is out

sometimes Clara leans her

head back and lets
the sun warm her face

from inside the house
I see them laughing
I see their mouths moving
up and down

back and forth

but I can't hear anything

my notebook is

still

empty

# Hair Dream #4

In this dream, I'm a hair stylist. A young girl comes into my salon, sits in the chair. She has no hair on her head. *Cut my hair into a bob, please,* she asks. I'm too embarrassed to tell her that she has no hair, so I pretend to cut her hair into a bob. I blow-dry her head. I even give her the mirror at the end, turn her chair around to show her the back.

# A Conversation

*Maybe you should just ask Clara*
Annie says after I tell her
about my
empty notebook

so one day I chew
my fingernails all the way down
until they bleed
and ask
Clara why her

hair falls out *I don't know*
she shrugs *it just does*

*stop being*
*so nosy*

and then she gets up and walks
out of the room

maybe I am
nosy maybe people aren't
supposed to talk
maybe the openings on our faces are
just for eating

maybe I want to know

too much
maybe I want to know everything
about Clara because she won't

tell me anything

I gather my courage to
ask my mom why
Clara's hair falls out

I have no more nails to
bite so I try to bite my toes
but can't reach them anymore

*I don't know*
*nothing wrong with her*
*don't talk about it*

*don't tell anyone*
she says

another notebook page

empty

# My Family

When Clara and I fight
my mom says

*you only have one family*
*one sister* but
that's my mom's

fault not mine

In social studies we are
learning about archaeologists and
when they dig they take
notes images soil samples
measurements looking for

anything something
but usually find nothing

I'm like them
I'm an archaeologist

in the barren cold of Saskatchewan

my lips are blue and cracked

I'm always looking for something

but I don't know what

maybe I'm looking for people

who talk about the rivers
that run beneath the earth how

they swerve to avoid each other
and then connect again

water is always talking
is always willing to

meld with other water no
matter where the other water

comes from

I wish someone would
save me from

all the

whispers

# Hair Dream #5

I'm braiding my own hair in this dream and I'm proud I can do this on my own—right hand over, then left hand over. I'm so excited to finish until I look behind me and my hair goes all the way down the entire street.

## The Doctors

The doctor looks
at Clara's head looks

at my mom

then back at Clara's head
sometimes the doctor glances
at me
I want to tell her

*it's not my fault*
*don't look at me*

but I always look down
or stare out the window

her eyes get squinty
as she gets close and picks at

Clara's head with little tweezers
it's so quiet that
I can hear everyone
breathing

I try not to look

I'm ready to write down what
the doctor says in
my notebook

but she doesn't really
say anything

so I draw her glasses that
have jewels on them

what I would do
to have
eyes like

diamonds

eyes that can cut
through
secrets

## Hair Dream #6

In another dream, I'm about to eat my dinner but when I look down, there's no food, just a plate of hair, little pieces with one green parsley leaf in the middle. I wonder if plated hair with seasoning will taste good. When I take my first bite, it tastes a lot like spaghetti but gets stuck in my teeth. My mom makes me finish the whole plate. After, I feel sick. But no one will take me to see a doctor.

# Doctors' Offices

More visits to doctors' offices
*Highlights* magazines are
my favorite
I can always find all

the hidden pictures

because it's for babies

I can never find real things

people always say *never*
*judge a book by its cover* or
*things are not always*
*how they seem* but if that's

true no one around us is

real nothing around us is

true everyone and everything

must be a lie who is lying and who is

telling the truth
who knows why
Clara's hair is falling

out someone who knows
isn't telling everyone else

who is that someone and why
won't they speak up

# Hair Dream #7

One day at school, everyone stares at my hair. Some people point and laugh. Others look so horrified they turn away. When I look at myself in the mirror, there are worms all over my hair, white worms. They are eating up all of my hair. From far away, it looks like I'm wearing a white hat.

# Bare

At night before Clara goes
to bed
her head is finally bare
no beret
no hat
nothing
I want to stare at

her bald spot that keeps
waving at me

I want to stand
on a chair over her head
and touch the short stubbles

I want to take notes while
I'm touching
put my pen behind
my ear

a researcher at
a science lab

but I try not to look because
she always snaps

*stop staring*

sometimes I catch
her touching the

hair with a few fingers
and shifting her hand as

if she's itching

sometimes I watch her
when she doesn't know I'm looking

the little hairs call her hand like a

foghorn she can't
see but can always hear

when she sees me
I turn away

# Fingers

My sister keeps her fingers off
her hair around my mom

as if she knows it will

only remind my

mom of the hair

the hair that never
seems to grow back

that refuses to grow back

the hair uses
the head

the head uses the

hair they need each other want
each other everything is about the hair

*take your medicine* my mom
says *eat these special vegetables*

*drink this special tea*
*use this new shampoo*

it's always the hair

about the hair talking about

the hair while not talking about the hair
looking at the hair trying to

pretend to not look at the hair I
can't help it I can't stop

thinking about the hair no one
says anything no

one really ever
says anything about anything

I hate the
hair and its

not growing I hate the little
pieces I find everywhere they
poke me in my
dreams like a cactus

# Hair Dream #8

I lean over and carefully pick out the little gnats in the baby monkey's hair. I must be a zookeeper. I untangle the baby monkey's hair. Her cute face winces as I pull. I'm excited because this is my dream job. I hear clapping but when I turn, I see my classmates outside of the fence looking at us and laughing, taking photos. I look down at my stomach that is covered with fur. I try and read the signs near the fence, but I can't read the words anymore.

# Brown Packages

My mom rips open
the brown package and
inside are smaller
blue boxes with black

Chinese characters that I can't read
boxes and boxes of
them from Taiwan

she opens them
and pours the dark brown
powder into plastic bags
she labels the bags with

more Chinese characters that
I can't read

I draw pictures of
the boxes in my notebook
try to look up the characters in
my Chinese-English dictionary

Clara eats
the powder one spoonful at
a time
her hair is

supposed to grow back
I watch her eat it every day

her face scrunches up like a
rotten apricot

the hair ignores

the powder

the powder ignores
the hair

no hair

grows
back

more empty
notebook pages

## *Maybe*

Maybe if I joined
the tennis team

just maybe

I can think about
something else besides

the hair
the hair
the hair
the
HAIR

maybe if I joined the
tennis team
the bubble would cover
me up

take me into a new
world where
people would watch me
hit the ball

stroke by stroke

where people would
look at how my feet move

where I could run back
and forth and get into
shape again

where my calves could be all
muscle

where I would no longer
have an

empty

face

# 4:

# face

# Bubble

On our way home
after playing tennis

Annie's cylinder of balls
falls out of her
bike basket

*wait* she yells
and I tighten my hands on
my brakes

before I can turn around
I hear the familiar sound of
rackets slapping balls
the sounds draw me in

I lay my bike on its
side and tiptoe into
the bubble

I love the smell of
the courts
the tennis balls
the sounds of
shoes squeaking

*Frances!*
it's Coach Meredith

my cheeks burn as
she waves me
over to her court

she hands me a nicer racket
and tells me to go
to the baseline before
I can say *no*

bouncy yellow balls
are speeding in my
direction with topspin
faster than
I've ever seen
before

I quickly start
hitting anything that
comes my way
balls fly by me and
smack against the plastic wall
behind me with loud thwacks

once in a while
I return a ball but
the balls keep
hitting the net

Coach Meredith tells
me to do this and
to do that and
to move my feet
and to bend my knees
and to follow through
and to turn my body
and to keep my eyes on
the ball and to point
to the ball
and I hear her and try
hard to do what she says
and suddenly my balls
start going over the net again
and again

we do this for what seems
like hours
she finally stops and
calls me over
to the net

she tells me when practice is
and to come three times
a week

I nod and she pats me
on the back with her racket

I try to return her racket
but she tells me to keep it
and to keep practicing

she moves to the next court
to help some other girls
who glance at
me curiously

Annie and I smile at the bright yellow
neon racket with a red *P*
in the middle all the way home

the tennis racket is my
face it is no longer

invisible

I don't tell my mom about

the bubble though

it's my secret

for

now

## Watching

I suddenly feel stronger
I suddenly feel like I can
do anything

almost anything

I decide to watch Clara
every day really carefully
to try and never

take my eyes off her
I decide to design
a science experiment

I start taking notes in my

notebook I count
the number of
hairs in her books

sometimes in places
where Nancy Drew is being
chased or there's danger

I see more bits of hair

I also learn Clara eats
a lot of Cheetos

she drinks
a lot of orange juice and
doesn't dilute it with water like she's
supposed to

sometimes she also

picks her nose and wipes her
finger on her books
I write down the names of those
books so I won't ever
read them

I watch her day and
night and
fill up my
notebook

with ideas

# Three Theories

After weeks of looking and
writing I begin to

notice how often

Clara scratches her head
I jot down the
number of times she touches her head

I'm up to seven times in an hour

she doesn't really notice me anymore
as I pretend to draw pictures

my head begins to spin with ideas
maybe her head is itchy so she

scratches and her hair falls out

but I wonder what makes
her head
itchy

I have three theories

I draw three arrows and write

*shampoo shrimp Cheetos*

how can I figure out which one is
causing her head to itch

I am committed to

this mystery

if I solve it
my false will become

true my invisible

will become

visible

# Experiments

On the first day I empty out my
sister's shampoo bottle fill it

with water add lemon add honey for
thickness add mint

*I like the new shampoo*
Clara tells my mom
but she still scratches her head

seven times an hour

on the second day
I tell my mom that Clara
wants her to make our favorite sweet-
and-sour shrimp for dinner

I watch Clara eat it
I even let her
have the last one

but after

she still scratches her head

the same number of times an hour

on the last day I take all the Cheetos
out of the house and throw
them into the trash
my sister doesn't
notice and eats

Fritos instead
I watch her and take
notes but still seven times an hour

I'm disappointed my experiments
don't work

I'm back to

square

one

# Library

I eat lunch
in the library at school most
of the time
because the cafeteria is so loud

and I'm afraid of not
finding anyone to sit with

I tear the edges off a bagel and
slip the bits into
my mouth
I look around the library
to make sure no one sees me

Annie has finished eating in
the cafeteria with her classmates
like she always does

she's looking at books now

I wave her over and
tell her about practice at
the bubble and
Coach Meredith
and how fun tennis is

*I told you so*
she beams

I also tell her about my
failed experiments

*how about hair books*
she asks
*have you looked for those*

Annie always thinks of the most
obvious thing

we scan the books on
the *H* shelf together

Annie is so close to me that
I can hear her
breathing and

smell her pizza lunch

*A HAIR BOOK*
I squeal

*shhhhhh*
the librarian raises
her eyes
at us
her glasses half down

we're afraid to search
on the internet

the librarian is always telling
us we're being *watched*

I hope the book will
change everything
unlock
all the locks of

my life

# Research

It turns out
there's a whole section of
books on hair

we read about the protein *keratin*
and how hair
skin and nails
are all made of it

we learn that *alopecia* describes
a person's thin or
balding patches

we learn about the parts of hair
such as the hair *shaft* that is the actual
hair *strand*

about the *root* and
the *follicle* or the place the hair
root grows from

then there's the hair *bulb* which is
below the *follicle* and that's where our
hair's color pigment or *melanin* is produced

*so that's why we have black hair* I say
*can we switch our hair bulbs*

Annie laughs
*I want a purple bulb*

I was thinking of a blond bulb but
maybe Annie's right

a purple bulb would be

much more

original

# Illnesses

Another book lists a bunch of possible
reasons for hair loss

*diabetes*
*thyroid disease*
*lupus*
*polycystic ovary syndrome*
*cancer*
*medicines*
*diet pills*
*hair chemicals*
*poor nutrition*
*disrupted hair growth cycle*

Annie and I read each aloud

then look at each other

blankly

how can we

possibly know

which one it is and
who can

help

us

# Laughing

Annie and I meet in the library
at lunchtime every day
to read about hair

we sit on the ground
cross-legged in the *H* section

but after a week we still
aren't sure how
to test these things

*we're hair experts*
Annie says one day

I laugh
*maybe we can set up a table*
*and label it*

*all your hair questions answered H-A-I-R*

Annie falls on her back while
she holds her stomach

*we're H-A-I-R for you*
she keeps laughing

if we solve this mystery
we'll be like *Sherlock Combs*
Annie snorts

I only half laugh because
we're stuck again

another dead end

the bell rings
Annie laughs all the way
down the hall

eventually I start
laughing again because
she's still laughing

I can't ever remember
laughing down the hall
like this before

my body loose

unaware of all the people
around us

this is how I feel on
the tennis court

maybe

this is what

happiness

feels like

## Something

For some reason Annie stops
coming to the library at
lunch I keep

looking through books about
hair and illnesses

I keep taking notes in my
notebook
which is now almost full

I search at home on my phone
but I'm scared someone will

look at my searches so I try
hard to stick to books

one day after school
I pass Clara's room and

she's crouched down

on her knees

shoving something
into a drawer she

turns and sees me
her face looks

surprised and caught as if

stealing something from
a store

I walk by slightly more
buoyant than

usual

something

has changed

ripples

on

a

still

lake

## Sleuth

*You're a snoop* says Clara
*stay out of my room*

now I want to snoop more
snoop for clues
no one calls

Nancy Drew
a snoop

they call her a sleuth
I'm a sleuth

one day Clara's gone
she's somewhere with my mom

my dad's somewhere in
the house or in the garage
I know he won't come find

me because he's still
working on the van

I tiptoe into
my sister's room
and open the drawer
I take a deep breath take
a last look around

start digging in the drawer
at the bottom in the back

under a stuffed banana is a
book the size of a thin Bible

I know what it is but I dare not
open it

I put it back
in the drawer

my hand is shaking
but my mind is leaping

it is absolutely silent in
the house

so silent I almost think
I have

disappeared

like steam

## The Diary

I can't stop thinking
about the diary
it calls me
sings
to me

glows through the drawer through
the walls into my blue room
with the blue wallpaper

during the day the diary doesn't

speak to me as much
but once in a while
when I'm at tennis practice

I hear a voice
it's not a human voice
it sounds raspy and
like a whisper
the voice tells me to
touch the diary's rough edges
to touch its smooth top to

feel its heat on my hands
I want to open it

to see the letters that melt like
wax I want to read

my sister's story I want to
hear someone speak to me

there are words in
this house
after all

# Open It

I tell Annie about the diary

*open it*
*and read it*
she says

*are you sure*
*isn't that bad* I say

*yes but we're trying*
*to solve a mystery*
she says

her eyebrows look cross
her arms at her side
palms open and up

*I feel weird*
*it feels weird*
I say

*what would*
*Nancy Drew do*
she says

I know what

she would do

Annie walks away
I see her

talking to
a group of girls

I don't

recognize

and a bee
stings

my

heart

# Open

One day the quiet is too
much it's so noisy
with quiet that I go
into Clara's room and

open the drawer I open

the diary and there they are again

small pieces of hair

everywhere on every page

stuck and flattened I hear
Nancy Drew's voice

*open it*
*open it*

*just*
*OPEN*
*it*

I sneak a look at
the words

*picked hair today*
*seven times tried hard not to pull*
*it out couldn't help it*

the next day

*tried hard not to pick hair again but*
*couldn't stop I pulled three hairs*

*out today I don't know why I can't stop*
*picking my hair*

I can't stop reading

the words carry me as if I am in
a fast flowing river

I want to

jump up and

scream

to punch through the

thick air of secrets
I want to tell someone
that my sister is not sick that
no one needs to pay attention to
her anymore that she is pulling
her hair out
that we are
the same
that we can all
go back to being normal
that I am an archaeologist who found
the prehistoric eardrum of
an extinct dinosaur and
now everyone can
stop whispering stop
pretending we are not okay
because
we
are
okay

*January 6*

*I will never stop.*
*Days gone without pulling: 3*
*I feel so bad for Frances. She just got yelled at for not looking at the audience during her concert. My parents are so MEAN.*

*During PE a bunch of kids stole my wig.*
*It's gone.*
*I'm so bummed.*
*What am I going to do?*
*They said it was a bet that my hair isn't real.*
*I didn't cry.*
*I wanted to cry.*

*January 7*

*Was doing so well and growing back but started picking again.*
*If I really wanted to quit, I could.*

*School is stressing me out.*
*Radmira Greenberg is so smart.*
*How does she do so well in school without studying?*
*Why do I always have to study so hard?*
*Why do my parents want me to get all A's all the time??*
*Why do I want to get A's all the time?*

*What makes me happy? Pulling.*

*January 8*

*I pull my hair. Yes I pull my hair. I want to stop pulling my hair.*

*Lisa Martinelli keeps asking me why I wear a hat every single day.*
*Why won't she leave me alone?*
*She sits next to me in math class and has the worst breath.*

*January 9*

*I hate myself sometimes. I hate my life.*

*I CAN STOP PULLING MY HAIR. I WANT TO STOP STOP STOP STOP PULLING MY HAIR.*

*Everyone's fighting again.*

*Frances is mad again because she's jealous of me.*

*No one pays attention to her because she's normal, not like me.*

*January 10*

*How do I stop? I can't. There's no healing just more pulling. I've been pulling for the last 3 hours. I keep telling myself just one more one.*

*Then I find 20 on the table.*

*Just one more.*

*Calming.*

*January 13*

*I once stopped pulling for 5 minutes.*

*No pulls today didn't even want to*
*so happy.*

*I'm the only one who pulls my hair.*
*The only one.*

*January 14*

*I'm SO excited! We're going to California!!!*
*We're going to drive across the country in the van!*
*I can't wait to get away from West Bloomfield.*
*I hate this town and all the mean kids.*
*I hate school.*

# The Wig Store

It seems like a long time has passed

but one day
we're at the wig store again

the wigs all look familiar
the faces holding
the wigs look familiar

I think one face
winks to me and says
*you're not alone little sister*
*you're not alone*

I somehow sense

that many sisters have been here before me
that many people like Clara have been here too

that the bodiless
heads must know a lot of secrets

Clara tries on
another wig in
the same bobbed style as before

I stare at the head with
the blue hair and
imagine
a world where everyone has

blue hair
where everyone has
the same body
the same face

and no one pulls
the blue hair out

and the blue-haired sisters
talk to each other in
a blue language

it sounds
like
paradise

*January 16*

*Now I have a huge bald thin patch on top of my head again. I have no more hair to pull. I pulled it all out.*

*Who would pull their hair out??*

*Grow pluck grow pluck grow pluck.*

*I hate mirrors.*

*January 25*

*How can I get away from it?*

*Is there a way to stop? I can't do this anymore.*

*I found a really good root.*

*A whole week of progress ruined in seconds.*
*Mom puts so much pressure on me.*
*Dad cut my hair again today.*

*He keeps telling me to start exercising and maybe my hair will grow back.*
*I wish.*
*Everyone is always arguing about my hair.*

*January 26*

*I like to roll the root between my fingers.*

*I hope I don't get it on the first pull.*

*January 27*

*Today I got a new canopy bed. It's really pretty and it's yellow. It also has flowers.*

*I also got a new pillow cover!*

*I love the canopy part of my bed.*
*It makes me feel safe.*

*February 16*

*This is the last piece of hair I will pull.*

*Frances is so lucky!*
*She is so perfect.*
*She's so good at tennis.*
*I'm not good at anything.*

*She doesn't pull her hair out.*

*Nothing bothers her.*
*She seems so strong.*
*Why me?*

# The Car

I'm surprised
I'm in Matt Demure's
car because I never ride in

anyone's car except my mom's car
my mom had to bring

Clara to another doctor's
appointment and I have to

go to a school event
Mrs. Demure turns the radio on

and starts singing as
loud as she can

Matt doesn't flinch just keeps looking
out the window as if

this is normal

I feel the heat on my face
expanding again

but it's not as hot as usual

something feels different

Mrs. Demure is jumping and
hopping and
clapping in
her seat I suddenly
want to tell everything to

this strange mom this
mom I desperately want

I know she would listen to me
I want to tell her about my sister
my sister's hair
my Chinese American family that is
mostly Chinese
about the kids at school who
tease me
how I love hitting
tennis balls as hard
as I can

but I sit quietly

hands on my lap

we stop at a red light
she sings and dances in her

seat turns the radio louder
I feel the car bounce

and shake
I'm moving as

the car moves
as if I'm dancing too

I hum and my mouth
moves a little to the words that

I'm surprised

I know

# Hair Dream #9

My black hair reaches my feet. All the kids from school follow me around each day, get on their knees, and beg to cut a small piece off. Sometimes I let them. One day I see them gluing some of the strands onto Clara's head.

*February 20*

*No more hair left to pull.*

*Frances is so lucky. Mom and dad leave her alone.*
*I wish they would leave me alone.*
*I wish Frances would leave me alone.*

*I wish I could tell Frances.*

# The Missing Wig

It turns out Josh had hidden
Clara's first wig in his room

they had moved it away
from the field when no one was looking

his mom had found
it in his room
he got in
big trouble

Josh and Steve
are gone from school for
two weeks
it's the best
two weeks of
my life

I'm not afraid to walk
down the halls at school

I don't have to take detours to
avoid their lockers

I can jog slowly during PE and look
at the trees and the birds and

not worry

the school returns
the wig with an apology letter from

Josh and Steve
their handwriting in even square blocks on
second-grade lined paper

Annie and I even get our
money back

the wig looks sad and

battered
someone had cut it
shorter and the ends are

all jagged and uneven
the top has been trimmed too

the wig now looks bald

*maybe the wig*
*needs a wig*
I say

Clara actually laughs

then we laugh together so hard that
our bodies shake and

tears come

down our faces

# Josh and Steve

Eventually Josh and Steve
return to school
and I can still
feel them in

the hallways but something
has changed

they don't tease me anymore
they don't look at

me anymore

out in the field they run
ahead and race with each other

chase the pretty American girls

the birds are more distant too
busy with their summer plans

distracted by their own routines

my head fills up with

the tingles before tears but
these tears are different

I take deep breaths and look up to
the sky my lungs fill up

with beating birds

they feel bigger as
if they've
grown
they try to

break

out

# Egg Rolls

I'm surprised
my mom asks Mr. Heart if she

can teach
everyone how to
make egg rolls

I help her carry in all the wrappers

meat and cabbage filling

electric wok

I avoid everyone's eyes

slink into my chair

my mom's face is pink and
she has small drops of sweat

on her nose
her English is hard
to understand but

everyone follows along as they watch
her hands
fill
fold and
roll

I glance over at Josh who is
working hard to keep his egg roll

from falling apart
his eyes stare hard at the egg roll
eyebrows angular

my mom calls me up to help
her fry

*lucky*
I hear Josh say

*I want to do that*
someone else says

my body straightens a little more and
I lift my head a little higher as

I help my mom
pat off the grease on the cooked
egg rolls with

paper towels and pass
the egg rolls out

when I get to Josh's desk
he looks excited

*thanks* he mumbles

I return to his desk with a
small red sack of
soy sauce

he nods and takes it from my hand while
his mouth is half open

I can see the bits of
egg roll in
his mouth

he is blowing with his mouth and fanning
with his hand

*you can't eat it too fast because the insides are really hot*
I'm surprised to hear my own voice

he winces and nods
gives me a thumbs-up

when my mom leaves she
turns around and

waves to me

smiles

she looks relieved

I wave
back

# Tennis Tournament

I'm surprised my mom tells
me she knows I've

been playing tennis at

the bubble

she says Coach Meredith
called to ask permission
for me to play
in a tournament and
told my mom how much

talent I have and how

hard I work

my mom looks angry and
she's yelling at me
but her lips are

curled upward slightly

*you have to work hard now*
she says
*you don't want to embarrass us*
*bring shame to our family*

I roll my eyes
as if I didn't already

know that

# The New Wig

It's almost the end of the
school year
finally

I imagine a whole summer

without Mr. Heart

a whole summer without Miss Beeoh
without Josh or Steve
or schoolwork or tests

maybe I can see Annie again
maybe Annie will want to be friends again

a whole summer of mowing the lawn up and down
overlapping just a little bit

a whole summer of
playing tennis at the bubble

and at the end of the summer
our big road trip
I don't know if I can wait
that long

I look out the window and see
Clara in her navy

beret placing her new wet wig on
the chair on the deck

I look up at the sky
a new set of clouds is out again spiraling and
shaping themselves

trying to be
permanent

Clara looks at a leaf lifting on
the chair but not blowing away

I want so badly

to say something to her

the urge like a hundred fists
punching me from the inside of
my chest

I want to tell her

*I know your secret*

# The Tournament

I'm excited the tennis
tournament is outside

the sun warms
my back

the wind blows
loose strands of hair
onto my eyelashes

I'm on the end court
I can see all the other girls
on the courts next to me

my new tennis friends wave
at me and wish me luck
I wave back and give
them a thumbs-up

I can see my parents
sitting on lawn chairs outside
of the fence

they wave
my dad smiles
I know my mom
doesn't smile because she's
nervous

Clara's standing
against the fence
wearing her white
baseball hat

I can barely see her

the fence divides
her into

tiny

diamonds

## Here

My opponent and I hit
ground strokes

we switch sides

we run up
and volley

she slams
an overhead down
for a winner

I serve two aces

we sweat
we grunt
pump our arms
pump our fists
dry off our sweaty rackets

my two feet land on the
ground
here

I'm nervous here but
feel whole

I can do things here
that I can't do anywhere
else

my opponents don't
make fun of me

my opponents look
scared of me

my opponents don't
think I'm ugly

my opponents think
my strokes are
beautiful

my opponents and I start
at the same place

here we're even
our scores start at
love love

and I feel like I can
lift the world with
my racket

# The Win

My parents don't hug me
after I win

but they stand across
from me
smiling
so I know they are proud

Coach Meredith comes
over and
gives me a high five

*Great job!*
she says loudly
*your daughter is doing*
*fantastic*
she tells my parents

she quickly trots to
the next court to
talk to one of my
teammates who lost her match

it no longer matters that
my parents don't give
me high fives

or that they don't cheer
loudly like the other parents

Clara hands me a
clean towel

and I understand
that's her way of
congratulating
me

I want to say
something back to
her but
I just say

*thanks*

# Letters

We're sitting at a large round
table at a Chinese restaurant as
large as a basketball court again

my dad is laughing so hard he
takes off his glasses to
wipe his tears

my mom's face is flush as she
chats with her Chinese friends

a big brown wet duck in
the center of the table
its curved neck shaped like

half a heart
fried colorful shrimp chips around
its body

Clara is on the other side of
the table

her bored face a mirror of
mine I catch her eye and

make hand motions two fingers
down means A

two fingers together curled
means B

my whole hand curved
means C

we struggle through our
own alphabet and make up

new ones like
a pointer and
middle finger intertwined is K

we send each other messages

*you eat the eyeball*
Clara spells out

I spell back
*no you eat it*

once in a while
my dad laughs so hard his
eyes shut
he wipes the sweat off
his forehead

we know we will be here for
hours because

they look

so happy

# Hands

I don't know why or
how but
maybe it's the
endless laughter
the Chinese words everywhere at
every table
in the air
that I can't quite
reach
or my good tennis matches
that afternoon or
my new friends

but my hands start

spelling out

*I*

*K-N-O-W*

in slow motion

*Y-O-U*

letter by letter

*P-U-L-L*

*O-U-T*

*Y-O-U-R*

*H-A-I-R*

the noise in the restaurant
seems to get louder and
louder

my dad's face seems to get
sweatier and sweatier

my mom looks more and
more nervous as she chats
with
friends

when I'm done I put
my hands down
on my lap

Clara puts her hands down
on her lap

she looks at the broken duck
on the table
half eaten

its neck has lost its
shape even its eyes
are gone

it seems like hours before
she stops staring
she lifts
her hands

*D-O-N-T*

*T-E-L-L*

her face looks urgent like

an umbrella hurrying
to
open
in a sudden
monsoon

I spell out

*O-K*

## Hair Dream #10

My hair has grown so long, I don't see its ends anymore. One day, I decide to follow my hair down the hallway out the front door, down the street, around the corner, around another corner. Sometimes I see a dog sniffing my hair. Sometimes a kid skateboards over my hair. I'm so busy looking down that I crash into Clara, who is also following her hair. When we reach each other, we are both holding the ends of our hair which are connected, one and the same.

# Never Again

After we finally get up and leave
the restaurant

my parents continue
laughing and talking outside in

the cold night
a late last cold snap
before full spring and summer

Clara and I wait
quietly in the dark van

light white clouds from our
breaths our bodies tight

shivering

I look at the light frost on the windows
small wispy frozen feathers

the muffled laughs outside

*they are so annoying aren't they*
Clara says suddenly

the darkness slips off of me like
a silk scarf

I am so excited to speak back
my words explode like a sneeze

*yes why do we always have to come to these boring dinners*

*I wish we could just stay home*
Clara says

*me too*
I answer back

*maybe when I get older I can just babysit you*
she says

we both burst out laughing because

we are nearly

the same

age

*hey great tennis matches today*
she says suddenly
*you've gotten so good*
*it's amazing you made it*
*all the way to the quarter finals*

pride blows up in my chest so
that I might burst like a piñata and

spill out my insides

we no longer hear
our parents and their friends
all we can hear is our chatting and
laughing

in the dark car
each looking ahead

leaned over
laughing
holding

our
stomachs

# Secrets

I still don't know why Clara

pulls her hair out

I still don't know
if she will tell my parents

but somehow

I know

it's not

my secret to

tell

somehow I know that

not even the snow can

bruise us anymore

because somehow

we know

we are each no longer

fully alone

# Author's Note

This story is based on my own childhood, growing up in West Bloomfield, Michigan. Many of the things in this story are true, but it's semiautobiographical because some of the stories are embellished and some of the smaller plot narratives are fictionalized. For example, I was never a great tennis player like Frances! That's just wishful writing. Also, much of this story is based on memory, and memory can be slippery.

It wasn't until I was in my thirties that I actually learned that my sister had been pulling out her hair the whole time (and still was) and that there is a name for it called trichotillomania, or "trich," thanks to Google. When I finally asked her about it, she was surprisingly open and told me she had gone to seek therapy and attended a support group for people with trichotillomania. She never told my parents. She was most surprised when she met people who pulled out their eyelashes and even eyebrows. I think trichotillomania can be a very embarrassing and shameful disease to its sufferers, and over time, I learned to respect that silence.

One of the hardest things about the disease for my sister and myself was growing up in an immigrant Chinese American family, a family that was not familiar with mental health issues such as trichotillomania, depression, anxiety, and OCD (experts believe that trichotillomania is a form of OCD, or obsessive-compulsive disorder), all things that can run in our family. My parents always did the best that they knew how, and they tried to help my sister in all the ways that they could while struggling to make a place in an unfamiliar and sometimes unwelcoming new country.

By writing this book, I hope that others who have trichotillomania or other challenges find the help that they need and eventually learn that there's no shame in having problems and that it can be a freeing experience to learn that a lot of other people have the same or similar problems.

I also hope that sisters, brothers, family, and friends know that they are not alone in dealing with the challenges surrounding families who have members who struggle with things such as trichotillomania. Mental health challenges such as trichotillomania, on top of the normal challenges of growing up, which sometimes might include bullying and grappling with identity, can be a lot to handle for kids and adults alike. And finally, I hope that people who don't know anything about trichotillomania learn something new through the experiences of Frances and Clara.

# Resources for Trichotillomania:

The Trichotillomania Learning Center: http://trich.org

Teens Health: http://kidshealth.org/teen/your_mind/mental_health/trichotillomania.html

Trich Stop: http://www.trichstop.com/info/general/trich-statistics

# Discussion Questions

*1.* Why do you think Frances feels so lonely?

*2.* Do you have any siblings or a cousin your age? Do you find yourself getting along with them?

*3.* Why do you think Clara doesn't tell anyone about her secret?

*4.* Have you, or a friend of yours, ever been bullied? What advice would you give to Frances when she faces a bullying experience?

*5.* Do you think the bullies in the book have changed? If so, how? If not, why not?

*6.* Why do you think Frances reads Clara's Nancy Drew books? She later treats Clara's illness like a mystery to solve. Why do you think Frances takes this approach?

7. How do you think Frances grows as a person throughout the book?

*8.* Frances relies on her friendship with Annie. How does their friendship change over time?

*9.* At the end of the story Frances and Clara seem to understand each other more clearly. How do you see their relationship evolving in the future?

*10.* Why do you think the book is written in verse/poetry? Did the form of the book have an affect on your reading process? Does it make you feel any different than reading a book written in plain text?

*11.* When Mrs. Chin visits Frances's classroom to make eggrolls, what did you expect to happen? Were you surprised by how she, Frances, and Josh reacted?

*12.* Think about the title of this book. What does it mean to you? Does the title have more than one meaning when it comes to Frances's life?

*13.* Frances's hair dreams can be scary, sad, and silly. These are the only times Frances's thoughts are expressed as plain text or prose. Why do you think the author made this choice?

*14.* Tennis is very empowering for Frances. Do you play a sport or have a hobby that makes you feel the same way? How does it affect your day-to-day life?